Mo Can't Go

For Harley

Published in 2015 by Pont Books, an imprint of
Gomer Press, Llandysul, Ceredigion, SA44 4JL

ISBN 978 1 84851 963 3

A CIP record for this title is available from the British Library.

This book is published with the financial support of the
Welsh Books Council.

Printed and bound in Wales at
Gomer Press, Llandysul, Ceredigion

Mo Can't Go

Rob Lewis

Pont

Mo is out in her car one morning
when all of a sudden it stops without warning.
Nothing happens when she turns the key.
She sits in her seat wondering what could it be.

Then she peers from above

and then from below.

But no . . .

Mo can't go!

Along the road comes
Megan the hen
She kicks the car and says
'Try again.'

The engine coughs and then stops dead.
Megan just watches and scratches her head.

Then they kick from the top and kick from below.

But no . . .

Mo can't go.

A mouse pops up and says 'I'll take a look.'
He climbs in the engine and checks every nook.
Mo turns the key as he fiddles about.
'It's still not working!' she says with a shout.

Then they check from above . . .

and then from below.
But no . . . **Mo can't go!**

A cat comes by and says 'What a day!
I've just got back from seeing Wales play.
Your car has stopped? Well fancy that!
Maybe one of your tyres is flat.'

'I'm sure they're fine,' Mo says in a grump,
as she gropes in the back and gets out the pump.

MO 1

Then they pump
from above

and they pump from
below.

But no . . .

Mo can't go!

'The car has stopped,' says Sian the sheep,
'because the road is much too steep.

They push and they puff and they pant all the way,
'til they get a good view of Cardiff Bay.
But when they get to the top of the hill,
the car rolls forward and then stops still.
So they push from above and they push from below.

But no . . .

Mo can't go!

'Shake the car!' says
Gwen the goose.
'Maybe something
inside is loose.'

Well, they rattle the windows and rattle the door.
They bounce on the seats and they stamp on the floor.

Then they shake from above
and shake from below.
But no . . .

Mo can't go!

'Out of the way!' says a tetchy toad.
'I once had a car and was king of the road.
I'll find the answer whatever it takes.
Stand aside while I look at the brakes.'

He looks from above . . .

and he looks from below . . .

. . . and then the car runs over his toe.

But no . . . **Mo can't go!**

Along the road strolls a friendly fox.
He carries a can and a metal box.

'I work in a garage, I'll find what's wrong,'
he says with a smile. 'It won't take long.'

Then he pokes and prods from above and below,
and after a minute he says to Mo . . .

MO 1

'I've found the answer! No need to thank . . .
You've got no fuel in the petrol tank.'

So he grabs his can and says 'Here you are,'
as he unscrews the cap and fills up the car.

The engine splutters,
and then it stutters.
The animals cheer
as Mo gets in gear.
At last she gets the car to start . . .

But then the whole thing falls apart!
Oh no!

Mo can't go!

'We'll get it fixed,' the animals say.
'Then you'll soon be on your way.'

Mo says 'Don't let's make a fuss.
Forget the car.'

'We'll go by . . . train!!!'